Fathers
Are Part of a Family

by Lucia Raatma

CAPSTONE PRESS
a capstone imprint

Little Pebble is published by Capstone Press,
1710 Roe Crest Drive, North Mankato, Minnesota 56003
www.mycapstone.com

**Library of Congress Cataloging-in-Publication Data is available
on the Library of Congress website**

ISBN: 978-1-5157-7463-1 (library binding)
ISBN: 978-1-5157-7472-3 (paperback)
written by Lucia Raatma

Editorial Credits
Christianne Jones, editor; Juliette Peters, designer;
Wanda Winch, media researcher; Laura Manthe, production specialist

Photo Credits
Capstone Studio: Karon Dubke, 7, 9, 11, 15, 21, Christianne Jones, 19; Shutterstock:
Angeline Babii, paper texture, digitalskillet, cover, Monkey Business Images, 17, Nikola Solev,
1, Romrodphoto, 13, Teguh Mujiono, tree design, Tom Wang, 5

Printed and bound in China.
010428F17

Table of Contents

Fathers

A father has children.

He is a parent.

Some fathers are called dad.

Some are called papa.

What Fathers Do

Madisyn's dad buys food.

Madisyn helps shop.

sale
4/1.00

Gina's dad is a doctor.

He works hard.

Nick and Noah's dad
likes art. He helps
the twins paint.

Mario's dad works at home.

He is a writer.

Molly's dads like to cook.

They make good food.

Lola's dad likes to play outside. So does Lola.

Fathers laugh.

Fathers love.

Fathers hug.

21

Glossary

doctor—a person trained to treat sick or injured people

papa—another name for dad

parent—a mother or father

twin—one of two children born at the same time to the same parents

Read More

Harris, Robie H. *Who's in My Family?* Somerville, MA: Candlewick, 2012.

Lewis, Clare. *Familes Around the World.* Mankato, MN: Heinemann-Raintree, 2015.

Simon, Norma. *All Kinds of Families.* Park Ridge, IL: Albert Whitman & Company, 2016.

Internet Sites

FactHound offers a safe, fun way to find Internet sites related to this book. All of the sites on FactHound have been researched by our staff.

Here's all you do:
Visit *www.facthound.com*
Type in this code: 9781515774631

 Check out projects, games and lots more at
www.capstonekids.com

Index